CONTENTS

Mr Grizley's Class ★

Cecilia Gomez

Shaw Quinn

Emily Kim

Mordecai Foster

Nathan Wu

Ashok Aparnam

Ryan Clayborn

Rahma Abdi

Bobby's

The Adventure of
PURPLE POTATO

Story

by Bryan Patrick Avery   illustrated by Arief Putra

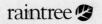

raintree

a Capstone company — publishers for children

Raintree is an imprint of Capstone Global Library Limited,
a company incorporated in England and Wales having its
registered office at 264 Banbury Road, Oxford, OX2 7DY –
Registered company number: 6695582

www.raintree.co.uk
myorders@raintree.co.uk

Designed by Dina Her
Original illustrations © Capstone Global Library Limited 2023
Originated by Capstone Global Library Ltd

978 1 3982 45303

British Library Cataloguing in Publication Data
A full catalogue record for this book is available from the British
Library.

Printed and bound in India

Nicole Washington

Alijah Wilson

Suddha Agarwal

Chad Werner

Semira Madani

Pierre Boucher

Zoe Charmichael

Dmitry Orloff

Camila Jennings

Madison Tanaka

Annie Barberra

Bobby Lewis

CHAPTER 1

Running Late

Bobby raced out of the copy shop and crashed into a teenage girl.

"Sorry about that," he said.

"Are you okay?" the girl asked. She was dressed in purple from head to toe.

Bobby nodded. "I'm all right," he said.

He noticed the girl's outfit and smiled. "You must like purple," Bobby said. "Look at this. I made it."

He handed her a copy of a small comic book.

"*The Adventure of Purple Potato*," she read. "Cool. We match."

Bobby grinned. "I'm Bobby," he said.

"My name is Ashley," the girl said. "My school is trying to raise awareness about helping people who are homeless."

She handed Bobby a flyer. He read it quickly.

"Wow," Bobby said. "I didn't know any of this."

"We need volunteers to spread the word," Ashley said. "Will you help?"

"Of course," Bobby said. "I'll even ask my class. I'm sure they'll want to help."

Ashley thanked Bobby for the comic book. He thanked Ashley for the flyer. Then, he hurried off to school.

CHAPTER 2

Attention, please?

Bobby made it to his classroom before the bell rang. He handed out his comic books.

"Amazing!" Shaw said. "I can't wait to read it."

Bobby remembered the flyer just as the bell rang.

"I've got one more thing," he said.

"It will have to wait," said Mr Grizley. "We've got a busy day today."

At breaktime, Bobby tried to talk to his classmates about the flyer.

"Can I show you something?" he asked Camila. She was skipping.

"Maybe later," Camila said. "I'm trying to break my record."

Bobby found Dmitry and Alijah playing tetherball.

"Can I talk to you two about something important?" Bobby asked.

"Sure," Alijah said. "As soon as our game is finished."

Nobody would listen to Bobby.

At the end of the day, Mr Grizley stopped Bobby on his way out of the classroom.

"I read the latest Purple Potato comic book," Mr Grizley said. "It's your best one yet. It looks like it's a hit with the class too."

"Thanks," Bobby said.
"Too bad I can't get them to
pay attention to this."

He handed Mr Grizley the
flyer about people who are
homeless. Mr Grizley read
the flyer.

"Don't give up," Mr Grizley said. "You just need to find the right way to tell the story."

CHAPTER 3

Purple potato to the rescue

That night, Bobby thought about Mr Grizley's advice. It gave him an idea.

Bobby drew a new Purple Potato comic. In it, the Purple Potato helped families who were homeless.

The next morning, Bobby arrived at school early. He carried a stack of new Purple Potato comic books. The class started reading them.

"Is this true?" Alijah asked. "There are more than one million children without homes in the country?"

Bobby nodded. "Yes, it's true," he said.

"I didn't know any of this," Camila said. "It says here that the number of children without homes is getting bigger every year."

"That's right," Bobby said. "That's why we need to do what we can to help."

Mr Grizley put a hand on Bobby's shoulder. "This is excellent work," Mr Grizley said.

"We need to help," Bobby said. "It's the only way we can make a change."

"Okay, class," Mr Grizley said. "Who wants to help people who are homeless?"

Every hand went up. Bobby beamed.

"Wow," Mr Grizley said. "You really got their attention."

"I just followed your advice," Bobby said. "I found the right way to tell my story."

LET'S MAKE A FLYER (AND TAKE A STAND)

Flyers are a great way to provide information. Let's make a flyer about a subject that's important to you.

WHAT YOU NEED:
- white or coloured paper
- felt-tips or crayons

WHAT TO DO:
1. Decide what subject you want your flyer to be about. Ashley's flyer was about homelessness, but you can choose whatever you want.

2. In large letters, write your subject at the top of the page. This is the title.

3. Below the title, write two or three facts about the issue. For homelessness, you could write:

- Homelessness means not having a home to live in.
- Lots of people without homes are families, including children.

   Ask your parents if you need help finding facts.

4. At the bottom, add a "call to action". This is just a way to help people know what to do next. You can ask people to tell their friends about the issue. You can also tell them where to go for more information.

That's it! Your flyer is finished. Feel free to make more copies and hand them out to friends and family. You're never too young to make a difference!

GLOSSARY

advice suggestions about what to do about a problem

attention careful listening or watching

awareness understanding or knowledge

homeless having no home

important having great meaning or value

volunteer person who does something to help, without being paid

TALK ABOUT IT

1. Ashley wanted to teach others about the troubles people who are homeless face. Why do you think it was important to her?

2. Why do you think it was hard for Bobby to get his classmates to listen to him? Why did using the Purple Potato help?

3. How do you think Bobby felt when his classmates didn't look at his flyer? What clues from the story and pictures tell you how he's feeling?

WRITE ABOUT IT

1. Ashley and Bobby wanted to help people who are homeless. Do you have a cause that you feel strongly about? What is it and why is it important to you?

2. Bobby's superhero character is Purple Potato. Create your own superhero and write a comic.

3. Ashley used a flyer with facts about homelessness to teach people. What are some other ways to spread a message? Make a list.

ABOUT THE AUTHOR

Bryan Patrick Avery discovered his love of reading and writing at an early age when he received his first Bobbsey Twins mystery. He writes picture books, chapter books and graphic novels. He is the author of the picture book *The Freeman Field Photograph*, as well as "The Magic Day Mystery" in *Super Puzzletastic Mysteries*. Bryan lives in northern California, USA, with his family.

ABOUT THE ILLUSTRATOR

Arief Putra loves working and drawing in his home studio at the corner of Yogyakarta city in Indonesia. He enjoys coffee, cooking, space documentaries and solving the Rubik's Cube. Living in a small house in a rural area with his wife and two sons, Arief has a big dream to spread positivity around the world through his art.